THE SPIRITS OF AOTEAROA

BY CORY VOSSPETER

THE SPIRITS OF AOTEAROA / NEW ZEALAND
By Cory Vosspeter

LOOK BEHIND THE VAIL AND SEE THE SPIRIT REALM

THE SPIRITS OF AOTEAROA / NEW ZEALAND

Copyright © 2025 by Cory Vosspeter

This book or parts thereof may not be reproduced in any form, stored in a Retrieval system, or transmitted in any form by any means, as electronic, mechanical, photocopy, recording, or otherwise, without prior written permission by the publisher.

This Book is protected by copyright laws.

This book contains biblical scriptures concerning the truth about the unseen world and it's spirit beings. Unless otherwise identified, Scripture quotations are from the New King James Bible (NKJ).

ISBN 978-0-473-72869-4

Contact: Cory Vosspeter at Email : CVosspeter@gmail.com

Table of Contents

Introduction

In Māori folklore fairies called patupaiarehe, also known as tūrehu and pakepakehā, these fairy like spirit beings are said to inhabit the forests and mountains of Aotearoa. It is said that such spirits only venture out at night or on misty foggy days. But I have found that photographing these spirit beings can occur during all hours of the day and night. I also photographed many fairy like beings near waterfalls. Some spirits are very small, others manifesting in the morning mist, just as the sun rises over the land.

This book is written to bring photographic evidence of the existence of the spirit realm and it's occupants. There are evils spirits lurking in forests, in volcanic areas, and in the waterways. All the spirits are hidden from human eyes to see but roam Aotearoa (New Zealand).

See the hidden spiritual world and it's occupants as I take you on a spiritual journey.

Note, it is very dangerous to go and seek these spirit beings out. I had special permission from the Lord God and through the guidance of the Holy Spirit, to photograph in the places He sent me. I only went to the places he showed me through dreams and visions, and took the photos he permitted me to take.

2

Thank You

Thank you, Heavenly Father for all things were created by you and for you. The seen and the unseen realms, the earth and the universe, all were created by you.

I also thank you Father God for the gifts you have given me. Let these gifts be used for your glory and for the advancement of the Kingdom of Heaven. Let your truth be known and your glory fill the earth. Holy Spirit please breeze upon the pages of this book, so that many will see, believe and be saved.

I like to thank my beautiful son Jacob-Isaiah for his love and support.

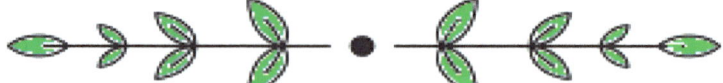

MY STORY

I was born in 1963 in Germany; at age three, I started seeing into the spirit realm. In 2005, my son and I moved to New Zealand. When we arrived in New Zealand, I started having dreams and visions of places where, in the past, blood had been spilled. The Word of God says, "The blood is crying out from the ground (Gen.4:10)." We contacted the local elders to gain inside. Once the places were found, we organized a small group of believers to accompany us. We anointed the grounds with oil, then, we prayed as instructed, according to the Word of God, releasing the curses from the land. The Lord instructed me to take photos before and after we prayed. After this, He then guided me to many more spiritual active places, which I photographed.

"Spirits of the Forest and Waterfalls"

"Little spirits in the Tree"

There were the Butterflies fly high up in the sky, these little people might catch a ride. In the trees these beings hide, away from most human eyes. Good dressed are some, with fancy clothes, hat, shoes and all .

"Spirits at the Waterfall"

"Spirits at the Waterfall"

As the early morning the sun rises near the waterfall, a gnome dressed in a black coat, going for a morning walk.

Original

"Spirits at the Waterfall"

As the early morning sun rises near the waterfall, a gnome dressed in a black coat, going for a morning walk.

(Added)

"Spirits at the Waterfall"

The midday sun shines at a nearby waterfall, the little beings bathing in the sunlight. (Original)

"Spirits at the Waterfall"

At the waterfall I photographed this black little spirit as it talks to an white fish.

Original

"Spirits at the Waterfall"

It was early morning just as the sun rose over the hills that were sur-rounding the waterfall, I photographed these little spirits. Seen here is an old lady dressed in a purple dress, holding a bucket. A yellow faced gnome walking nearby. A spirit dressed in white, it is sitting on the near-by tree. And flying spirit and a spirit man.

"Shadow spirits at the Waterfall"

Standing near the waterfall, in the shadow of the trees I hide. Can you see me with your eyes?

These are shadow spirits, they are spirit beings that look like shadows, but are real spirit beings. I was amazed to find them on one off my photographs.

"Shadow spirits at the Waterfall"

Standing near the waterfall, in the shadow of the trees I hide. Can you see me with your eyes?

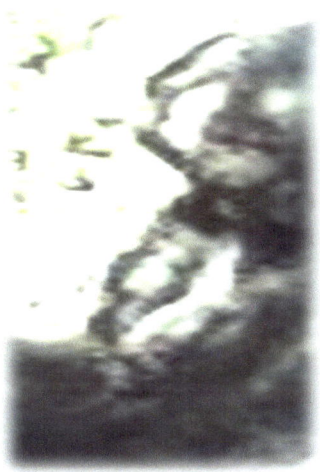

"Spirits at the Waterfall"

All in white I am dressed, black hair so fair, here I stand.

I am a gnome, I wear a hat, pants and boots too. I stand near the waterfall , can you find me ?

"Spirits at the Waterfall"

This spirit person was looking up at me as I photographed the nearby wa-terfall. Then in the waterfall a spirit of a women can be seen.

"Spirits at the Waterfall"

When the sun comes out during the day the little people come out to play.

"Spirits at the Waterfall"

In between the foliage three little man, hide, they are not taller than one of our fingers. Can you see them?

"The Garden Giant"

The Garden Giant (original)

"The Garden Giant"

"The Garden Gnome"

In the Garden they are seen, between the trees and the flowers purple sweet and fine, let this be a swing of mine. Between the green leaf's the fairies keep watch, far away from a humans touch.

Who can see me I may ask?

"The Flower Fairy"

In the Garden they are seen, between the trees and the flowers purple sweet and fine, let this be a swing of mine. Between the green leaf's the fairies keep watch, far away from a humans touch.

Who can see me, I me ask?

"The Fairy Tree"

This is what I call the Fairy tree. In this tree a dimensional doorway opened, and I photographed a different dimension. Here you can see little houses and the little spirit beings that live there.

This is what I call the spirit tree. In this tree a dimensional doorway opened, and I photographed a different dimension similar to our own.

"The Fairy Tree"

"The Fairy Tree"

In the world not known to humans and hidden high up in a tree, far from the human eyes to see, lays the world of the little spirit beings we call fairies. In a different dimension, quiet like our own world we see; little houses and fences and fairy people.

25

"Fairy of the Night"

In the darkness of the night, the fairies try to hide. Deep in the forest I shown a light, the fairies I surprised. (0riginal)

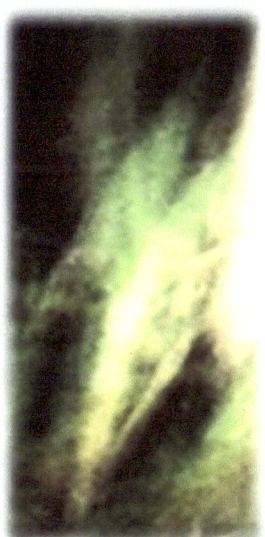

"Evil spirits of the earthly realm"

"Evil spirits lurking in the Forest"

A misty spirit is seen lurking between the trees.

"Evil spirits lurking in the Forest"

A surrounded by a mist this spirit is seen lurking between the trees.

"Evil spirits lurking in the Forest"

"Evil spirits lurking in the Forest"

This spirit person is wearing a long coat and a cone hat, as he walks towards a dimensional doorway. He is in spirit form.

"The Volcanic Zone"

At the Volcanic Zone of New Zealand, I photographed a shift in the dimension, that lies between our world and the spirit world. In this photo a spirit animal, a gnome with a sword and skeleton demons can be seen. The Dimensional Shift and spirit beings (orig.), skeleton demon, spirit animal, gnome with sword.

"The Volcanic Zone"

Seen here is a gnome with a sword.

Added

"Evil spirits of the Mist and Water"

"Spirits of the Mist and Water"

A gate of Hell where the mud pools sousing many travellers, there I found these evil spirits.

"Spirits of Mist and Water"

At a lake where children play, there I found evil lurking on the waters edge. (Original)

"Spirits of Mist and Water"

(Added)

"Spirits of Mist and Water"

At a lake where children play, there I found evil lurking on the waters edge. (Original)

"Evil spirits of the Air"

"The Dragon spirit of the Air"

(added)

The Dragon/Serpent

"Spirit Animals"

"Strange spirit animal at the Waterfall"

At the waterfall in the afternoon sun, lays a very unusual animal.
A bird like creature with the head of a goat, is resting here.

"Big Spirit Cat"

On a nice sunny day we visited this waterfall, I took some nice photos and noticed that I had photographed this spirit cat.

Between the trees I hide, can you see me?

"Spirit Cats"

These spirit animals have died due to a sudden volcanic eruption.

Can you see the spirit cat's ?

"Spirit Animals"

These spirit animals have died due to a sudden volcanic eruption.

Can you see the spirit, deer, dog, cow and others?

Teachings

Questions and Answers

Are these spirit beings just nature spirits or demonic entities?

Here are examples that open doors to the demonic realm.

Demonic doorways are opened through Idol worship, places that were dedicated to Idols, demons and evil spirits.

Places where blood had been spilled, through murder and blood sacrifices through Occultic practices.

Reading New Age and other spiritual books, watching horror movies, martial art practices, yoga practises and alike.

Tarot card reading, Ouija board, Dungeons and Dragons game, and alike, and taking drugs. Having Idols in your house, like Buddha statues pictures of foreign god's and alike, and the believe in crystal and spirit healing, will invite evil spirits and demons into the house. And Necromancy, calling upon past loved once.

"Biblical scripture references"

Demonic spirits and their nature:

The Word of God describes many kinds of demonic spirits that are under satanic control. There are many different demonic spirits have different assignments. Demons are morally evil in character and wickedness. **(Matthew 12:22-30).**

Genesis 4:10 - "The voice of your brother's blood is crying to me from the ground.

Exodus 20:3 - 5 - "You shall have no other gods before Me. "You shall not make for yourself a carved image, any likeness of anything that is in heaven above, or that is in the earth beneath, or that is in the water under the earth. You shall not bow down to them nor serve them. For I, the Lord your God, am a jealous God, visiting the Iniquity of the fathers upon the children to the third and fourth generation of those who hate Me.

Isaiah 45:20 - Who carry the wood of their carved image, and pray to a god that cannot save.

Demonic spirits (to name a few).

Unclean spirits - Luke 11:24 - 26 What happens when an **unclean spirit** returns after being cast out of a person? "When an unclean spirit goes out of a man, he goes through dry places, seeking rest; and finding none, he says; "I will return to my house from which I came." And when he comes, he finds it swept and put in order. Then he goes and takes with him seven other spirits more wicked than himself, and they enter and dwell there; and the last state of that man (person) is worse than before it got cast out.

Spirit of Infirmity - Luke 13:11 - 13 And behold, there was a woman who had a **spirit of infirmity** for eighteen years, and was bent over and could in no way raise herself up. But when Jesus saw her, He called her to Him and said to her," women, you are loosed from your infirmity. And He laid His hands on her, and immediately she was made straight, and glorified God.

Seducing spirits - 1 Timothy 4 :1 - 4 The Great Apostasy. Now the Holy Spirit expressly says, that in latter times some will depart from the faith, giving heed to deceiving spirits and doctrines of demons, speaking lies in hypocrisy, having their own conscience seared with a hot iron, forbidding to marry, and commanding to abstain from foods which God created to be received with thanksgiving by those who believe and know the truth. For every creature of God is good, and nothing is to be refused if it is received with thanksgiving.

Demonic spirits (to name a few).

Familiar spirits - 1 Samuel 28:7 - 25 Then Saul said to his servants; "find me a woman who is a medium, that I may go to her and inquire of her." And his servants said to him; "in fact, there is a woman who is a medium at En Dor." In the end, God's judgement falls on Saul for going to a medium.

Divination spirit - Acts 16:16 - 19 Now it happened, as we went to prayer, that a certain slave girl possessed with a spirit of divination met us, who brought her masters much profit by fortune telling.

Evil spirits - Luke 8:2 - and certain women who had been healed of evil spirits and infirmities. **Acts 19:12** - So that even handkerchiefs or aprons were brought from his body to the sick, and the diseases left them and the evil spirits went out of them. (**Judges 9:23, 1Samuel 16:14,23, Luke 7:21, 8:2, Matthew 15:22**)

Scripture Reference:

Zechariah 10:2 - For the idol's delusion; the diviners envision lies and tell false dreams; they comfort in vain. Therefore, the people went their way like sheep; they were in trouble because there was no shepherd.

Galatians 5:19-21- The acts of the flesh are evident: sexual immorality, impurity and debauchery; Idolatry and witchcraft; hatred, discord,

jealousy, fits of rage, selfish ambition, dissensions, factions: and envy, drunkenness, orgies, and the like. As I did before, I warn you that those who live like this will not inherit the Kingdom of God.

Those sins lead to spiritual death and eternity in hell, being separated from a loving heavenly Father.

Psalms 135:15-18 - The nations' idols are silver and gold, made by human hands. They have a mouth but cannot speak and eyes but cannot see. They have ears but cannot hear, nor is there breath in their mouths. Those who make them will be like them, and so will all who trust them.

Isaiah 45:20 - Gather together and come; assemble, you fugitives from the nations, ignorant are those who carry about idols of wood, who pray to gods that cannot save.

<u>Conclusion</u>

In conclusion I believe that most of these spirit beings in this book, are demons and found in the places that are spiritual unclean. In these places blood had been spilled through human sacrifice and wars.

Here we see demons in spirit form, they have a spirit body. They see, walk, smell, taste. And as you can see, they have hairs, and a beard, and wear clothes. So are angels in spirit form, they are clothed in the glory of God. We will be in spirit form when our body dies and we pass over into the spirit realm. The spirit realms, heaven and hell are real places.

Please stop with the wickedness, lying, unforgiveness, stealing, adultery, fornication, watching porn, and such, witchcraft of all sorts, worshipping idols. Please repent, turn away and turn to the only person who can save your soul, Jesus Christ.

 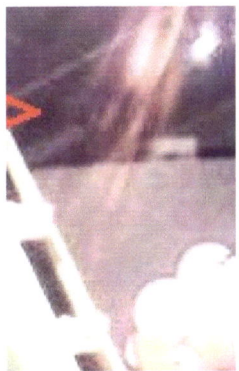

Give your Life to Jesus Christ and be eternally saved

Salvation Now. After we die, we will be in our spirit form and if we are not born again, our spirit body has not received the forgiveness and Salvation of Jesus Christ, we will join the demons in hell.

Salvation Prayer: Father, please forgive me my sins, wash me in the blood of your Son Jesus Christ, who died on the cross for my sins and died and rose again. Jesus be my Savior, I give you my life, come and be my Lord and lead me by your Spirit I pray, Amen.

Salvation is received by faith through grace. He loves us so…